SMALL CHANGE

SANDRA HUNTER

GOLD LINE PRESS 2016

SMALL CHANGE

Published by Gold Line Press

http://goldlinepress.com/

Gold Line titles are distributed by Small Press Distributions

This title is also available for purchase directly from the publisher

http://www.spdbooks.org

800 869 7553

Library of Congress Cataloging-in-Publication Data

Small Change / Sandra Hunter

Los Angeles, CA : Gold Line Press, 2016

Library of Congress Control Number 2016936905

Hunter, Sandra

ISBN 978-1-938900-20-4

FIRST EDITION

Contents

SMALL CHANGE

30 BELOW

I don't want to go. Hamad smells bad and he will push me against the dirt walls, and he will go far ahead and leave me behind with the cold earth smell in my nose and not knowing if I can go on. Hamad knows I hate the tunnel even though I have never been inside.

The other carriers, all adults, are calm. They trick us, the younger boys like my brother, Abir, into doing the hard work. But when the tunnel opens the young ones are sent home. Go and rest, they say, here is fifty dollars. That's what they did with Abir, but he is tall and even though he is only eighteen he insisted to carry. They said: He is now a man. The father isn't working. Someone must feed the family.

Abir brings cigarettes and oils and medicine and coat hooks; all the things we used to buy in our shops. Everyone crowds around Abir as he comes out of the tunnel with microwave ovens and brazil nuts and dresses the colors of sunset. It's like a feast day. One day I will buy my little sister a sunset dress and she will stand on the roof top in the evening and you won't be able to tell where the sky ends and her dress begins.

Abir says digging the tunnel made him calm. It isn't a job that goes quickly. It has its own rhythm, he says, like this: dig and dig and dig and *push* the dirt backwards. It took one year to dig through from our side into Egypt where those dogs crouch, waiting for our kalishnikovs. A year of sneaking out before dawn, three streets across and four houses down, sneaking back after dark. Abir's eyes changed. He wore dark glasses and my father was angry. *So now you are an American gangster*. But Abir was only thinking of going into the hole and how he must not touch the electricity.

And now he is sick. *We can't lose this job, Sami. It's up to you*. My father hasn't worked at the bakery since those dogs cut off access. *My bakery. Gone*. My father's hands, once always covered with flour, are bare and empty. He sits, hands hanging between his knees, no longer knows what to do with them. But at least he has his hands. Khalid-across-the-street had his hands blown off when he picked up the yellow bomb. Stupid. Everyone knows to leave those things alone. I shouted for him to stop. For a moment the world went deaf and Khalid flew one way and his hands flew the other. He is lucky it is the hands only.

I am thirteen. Abir is five years older than me. He is big from all the digging. I am thin. His nose is much bigger and his skin is terrible from the acne. But I am the only one who can go. Abir says I am now the man in the family, so I will wear his shirt and jacket and his dirt-grey pants that I will tie with a string around the waist. It feels like I am already inside the tunnel and everything smells of darkness when I shrug the shirt over my head. I put on his dark glasses and look in the mirror. Abir looks back. I will wear the glasses and smoke a cigarette until I am at the mouth of the tunnel. Abir has told the guards on duty that I am coming. I will wrap his green and white scarf around my head, throw the cigarette to one side like I don't care that it is half-smoked. My mother knows all of them, these guards. She knows all their families, has given food to many of them, dressed their wounds from gunshots or other accidents. She has gone to the funerals of their brothers and fathers and uncles, after the killings that happen almost every month. They will watch over me as I climb down next to the two winches, one to send boxes into Egypt and the other to pull boxes back.

As I climb down I think, *Now it is my first time*. I won't think about how deep I am going. Nine meters. Hamad is already crawling ahead, following the boxes as they are winched through. Abir told me, *Don't think about it. Just go*. It is easy for him. He has dug this tunnel so he is used to it. But it is very small in here. The tunnel roof is barely two feet above me and three feet wide, lined with boards and wooden supports. I could almost crouch and walk through but I am afraid of the electricity. It is a good thing I am so thin.

The tunnel owner says it is safe. He says he stays in the shaft all the time. He bids me *go well*. I don't think about what will happen if he goes to lunch or to the bathroom, or who will be there if the electricity goes out, or what we will we do with the boxes if we are left in the dark. Or if I touch the electricity. These questions are for babies.

Abir, hard lean arms, long muscled back, is strong like this tunnel. I can see Abir there, just ahead, peering over his shoulder as he digs up more dirt. *Come on, Sami. Get going*. So Abir might be older but he's not a fast runner like me. He can wrestle anyone but he can't run for more than twenty yards without coughing. Too much hookah, I tell him.

It is cool down here. That is good. Much better than being up there in the heat. *Pleasant*, Abir calls it. It might be if I don't think about the nine meters of earth above my head. Some people say they can smell the water. I get only the red smell of earth, something like blood the way it catches in the throat.

Some of these tunnels you can stand up in. They say there's one you can drive a car through. That makes me laugh. A car driving underground, shaking the dirt walls so the whole tunnel falls down? What fool would do that? Even so, I would like to drive in that car. I would put my foot down so hard that we'd be at the other end before they'd finished giving us Allah-Go-With-You.

Hamad's strong shoulders as he lowers himself into the shaft, his eyes bright and his hands grasping the rope. It is my turn and even though I have promised myself I will go quickly, just like Hamad, I am scared and my hands grip the rope. The men call out to remind me to keep going down and even when I reach the bottom, I cannot let go. I can hear Abir, *What are you waiting for?* I must show I'm brave, like Abir. I kneel down and enter the tunnel which is about four feet high. Far ahead, I can only just see the soles of Hamad's feet, pale fish swimming ahead of me. The electricity crackles and buzzes. Keep low, keep away from the wire.

This is nothing like a grave, even though Abir has joked about it. Does a grave have electricity? Does a grave see goats being pushed through, smell the oranges, hear the rattle of plastic pill bottles we will bring back? This is a doorway to life. And anyway, Abir says our tunnel has more wooden supports so it is more secure than others. It is just near Salah Al-Dain Gate in Rafah — too far south for those Israelis to bomb. Sometimes the Egyptians send death into our tunnels with gas or even water so that people will drown. I used to think the Egyptians were our friends.

Okay. I admit I am scared of the gas. You can't smell it. It creeps up and sinks into your lungs and then you are dead. Can you go to Jannah, paradise, if you are gassed in a tunnel while you are smuggling? Surely it is a greater sin to kill someone. Perhaps the Egyptians can argue that they are only trying to stop us, so if we die it is by chance and not intention. Is accidental death a smaller sin than smuggling? We wouldn't smuggle if the borders were open. So we are forced into sin because of the Israelis, and the Egyptians are forced into sin because of us.

Abir says he doesn't believe in the rivers of milk and wine and honey in paradise. But even so I still pray for Abir to be there with me and taste the many fruits that we won't have to smuggle. I used to wonder what would happen if a goat or a sheep fell into the river of milk.

Would it still be pure and clear? Perhaps the goats and sheep will be clean all the time so it won't matter. It must be a terrible thing to drown in honey.

A faint, sweet smell comes, and I cry out and put my hand over my face. Is this the gas? Will I die now? I will never see my mother or father again. I will never see Abir or my sisters. I have failed the family. I will surely not go to Jannah now. There is a bright light coming toward me. Death is coming fast so I must prepare. Oh Allah, forgive me for my sins of smuggling and failing my family and ... The smell becomes very bad and something hits me on the side of the head. It is Hamad who wants to know if I am going to cry like a baby in the tunnel forever while he does all the hard work. Hamad says that if he didn't fear the wrath of Allah then he would call down curses from his dead mother on me.

He has to struggle to turn around again and I can see that by coming back he has even left the boxes for me. But then he has no choice because he may not abandon his family. It's in the top ten major sins. I don't like Hamad, but he is my third cousin and it's because he talked to the tunnel owner that I was allowed to make this trip instead of Abir. So, I must do as he says. As he squirms around to face forward, he reaches one arm and pushes my head hard against the tunnel wall. I don't cry out.

Hamad goes quickly ahead to catch up with the boxes and I wait until I can't smell him anymore. The sweet smell comes back and I realize that it is Abir's aftershave that lingers on the scarf. I want to yell ahead to Hamad but I don't think he will be interested.

Soon it is just like before. No sound except the faint shuffling of Hamad ahead, buzzing of the electricity, my breathing, and the scrape of knees and hands against dirt. I try to think of good things, like beating Yousif at soccer. He thinks he's so good because he can kick hard. Everyone knows there's more to soccer than kicking.

Suddenly, I realize Hamad has committed the number one sin: he has prayed to his mother. But then, he didn't really pray to her because he fears Allah. But he almost did. And it is my fault. If I hadn't been so stupid about the gas I wouldn't have cried out and Hamad wouldn't have been forced to come back and become angry with me. So, really, it is my fault; I have committed the number one sin. I immediately pray for forgiveness. Allah will know I didn't mean any harm. There are sins of intention and mistake, and mine is just a mistake. And, I quickly add, Hamad, too. He didn't mean it either.

What is it about the tunnel that makes me think so much about sin? I don't usually think about it at all except if I forget afternoon prayer. I play soccer with Yousif, Basim and Raed, or we listen to American rock music. We spend most days on the other side of Rafah in the bombed out shopping center. Mama still thinks I go to school. All we talk about is digging and how we're going to make the next big tunnel.

The tunnel is 2200 feet long but it feels like I have been crawling for days. When I see the daylight at the other end I'm so happy, but it is so bright. I think these Egyptians must have brought a spotlight. Now I can understand why Abir had to wear dark glasses.

I crawl up the ladder and hands reach down to lift me out. I breathe in the fresh warm air and everything is so full of color. Like so many others back in Rafah, the shaft opening is in someone's house. A tall cupboard with a mirror sprays silver light. I strain to see the names of the books on the long bookshelf. These are rich people. Music is playing very loud and I think I recognize the song when I see the men are laughing at me. Hamad is telling how I cried out like a baby. Someone almost like Abir's age says, Don't worry. They are laughing now but everyone has fear of the tunnel.

Even though Hamad is also laughing, he is angry and he cuffs me hard around the head, What will I do with this boy? He should stay with the women.

The others add comments and I shrug to show I don't care even though I wish Hamad could say I was brave to come anyway. I don't have a passport so I must stay here. Abir told me I mustn't be caught. I will not think about being caught.

The men are working quickly, lowering the boxes that we must take back through tunnel. They tie them onto the platform that will run back along the pulley system. Hamad will go first and follow that one. I am to wait and then follow with the cow. This is a punishment for me because the cow is much more work. I will have to make sure it doesn't thrash around and break its legs. I don't know what I can do to calm a cow. I wish they had put it to sleep.

Hamad throws a look at me. I feel its edges across my face like my father's shaving razor. You are a problem.

I will learn.

He shakes his head, What use is learning if you are dead?

I will do better, Hamad. I promise.

The one who is Abir's age says, Come.

We go to the kitchen and I wait while he goes out. Outside the window is Egypt. Grey dust blowing. A girl in a burqah walks past. I thought the girls would wear skirts and t-shirts like I have seen on television. Two men sit at a wooden table that tilts. They have glasses of tea. Near them, a woman ties up a bundle of clothing and shifts it onto her head. But, still, here I am in a foreign country. Egypt. It sounds so foreign in the mouth, like a strange fruit.

The one who is Abir's age comes back with a plastic box of milk. He pours some into a bottle and screws a teat on top. He hands it to me and lifts his chin indicating that I must feed the calf. I go back to the other room where the calf, tied to a table, is making little leaps at anyone who goes past. Maybe someone will buy this one and keep it, or maybe they will slaughter it for a feast. It is very small, perhaps only a week old. It tugs at the bottle and I have to put a hand on its back so it doesn't tug itself over backwards. The calf continues to tug when the bottle is empty but there is no time for more milk. Hamad should be close to the other end and we must leave.

The men tie a rope around the calf and carry it over to the shaft. They lower it slowly, like a sack of flour. It is crying and its eyes are rolling. I can tell this is not going to be an easy journey for us. They will turn the power off so the calf can walk through the tunnel safely. This is good since we won't have to worry about touching the electricity. But there will be no light. I will have to persuade the calf through the tunnel.

I climb down the ladder into the shaft, wondering if Hamad will complain to my brother about me. The calf is whimpering. I haven't heard this sound before; this one is crying almost like a puppy. I put a hand on its head. The calf pushes at me and licks my hair with its slobbery tongue. I pull away and talk to it, We are going through the tunnel. You have to be calm. Don't go breaking your legs or they'll just kill you on the other side. We're going to be fine. You see? I have a flashlight.

I shine the light away from the calf and it stares at the black hole ahead. The men call to me. They are shutting the power off. If Hamad is still in the tunnel they will have to pull the boxes along from the other side. But I cannot think about Hamad. I have to ease the calf into the tunnel. It moves forward but slowly. It is crying again. I crawl behind and talk to it. What should I say? I had better not mention its mother or it will be even sadder. I talk about the grass that it will eat in Rafah, about the sky that is so much bluer, and the nice bucket of water it will have to drink. I talk about the kind family it will live with until I remember that it may end up on someone's feast menu.

My flashlight shows the bumpy ceiling and walls, and throws jumping shadows ahead of us. The calf begins to panic and kick. One hoof catches me on the ear and it is like a bomb has exploded. I clutch my ear and switch off the light. Immediately, the calf is quiet. I realize we will have to go through the tunnel in the dark. But the calf will not move. I try pushing it gently, but it digs its hooves in, its bony bottom pressing against my head. I try to push more forcefully but it releases a jet of urine and I am drenched. I am annoyed with the calf even though I know it's just a baby.

There is only one thing to do: I must lead the calf through. It can trot after me while crawl on my hands and knees. But the tunnel is too narrow for me to squeeze ahead of the calf. So I lie down and pull the calf on top of me. I have to be careful, holding it close in case it panics and breaks a leg. The calf is not cooperative and I am kicked in the face, throat, elbow, chest, stomach, privates, shins and ankles, but I finally manage to get it behind me. We breathe together in the dark. It starts to crawl on top of me again and I struggle onto my front and begin crawling ahead, calling as I go. It follows for a little, its nose bumping my heels. Then it stops again. I realize that it could easily run back to the other end of the tunnel.

We must have been down here for almost half an hour and we have barely moved twenty feet. I have to think of something to calm the calf. I remember the music that was playing from the Egypt end and I try to sing the tune as I crawl along. I can only do la-lee-la-la but the calf doesn't seem to mind.

Just as I am wondering if making the calf go through the tunnel is a sin it starts butting me from behind. I try moving faster but the calf continues to trot along and butt me. I scramble along and I can hear the calf's feet and feel the hard little head against my feet, my thighs, my rear end. I stop to discuss this butting business with the calf. But the calf is happy for an opportunity to nuzzle my face and chest, and licks my ear, the sore one.

I know if I try to go behind the calf again, we will make no progress at all. I have to put up with the herding. We continue, me crawling ahead as fast as I can go, and the calf butting me along.

The rumbling sound, I think, is the electricity. I am angry that they would turn it on while we are still down here. I reach back to grab the calf but there is no buzzing, no flickering light and then I know exactly what it is. It must be quite far away, I think. If it was closer we'd already be dead. Earth shakes off the walls. I hold the calf close to me and it sticks its head under my arm. I say, sshh, sshh. It will be all right.

Ahead of us, towards the Rafah side, small pebbles of earth begin to slide down the narrow walls. We have to go back the other way. I push the calf but it wriggles back under my arm. There is no time to coax it. I have to go through being kicked in the head and chest and stomach and legs so I can crawl in front and lead it back to Egypt. All the time the calf is crying, this terrible hopeless sound.

We are going fast, fast, but not fast enough. Finally, I hear faint shouting from the Egypt end and I think I can see the light. The wall boards are groaning and jostling as we grab our way over the shifting earth. I can't tell what is ahead and what is behind. The calf's head is right up on my back like it wants a piggy-back.

I can hear the men's voices more clearly and we can't be more than ten feet from the light when there is a hard, fast series of cracking thumps and the tunnel above us collapses. I hold the calf under me. It is going to die of fright and that is better than dying of suffocation. The hailing clods of earth beat me over the head and back and shoulders just as two of the tunnel wall-boards fall together creating a temporary tent above us. I know this small refuge will also break. I don't want to die. Forgive me for my sins. And please bring Abir with me to the rivers in paradise. And spare the calf, too, even if it just an animal.

The earth is folding us in to itself. The quick warmth of the calf breathing beneath me. I try to shift so I am not lying directly on top but the earth presses me down and down. The breath pulsing quickly from the calf beneath me. I don't feel anything else, just the small in and out of our breaths. Soon I will not be able to breathe. Soon we will both be still. I don't want to know when the calf dies.

Something smashes into the boards and I am jabbed hard in the back. It smashes again down on my shoulder and I am being cut in two. Shouting and earth pushed into my eyes and ears and voices calling out, He is here! He is here!

We are birthed back into the loud world. We are choking, blinking, and blind from the sudden light, and so weightless we could fly. There are cheers and hugging and they bring water. Someone tries to take the calf from me, but I hold on to it. We are carried to a different room. Someone peers into our eyes and ears and throats. We are full of tunnel. Abir's shirt is full of blood. Someone says I am lucky that it is only cuts and bruising. It hurts to breathe and the breathing that was so small under the ground is still small up here. My shoulder is bandaged and someone holds a stethoscope to my ribs. They say maybe cracked ribs but I should be glad my lungs are working.

Someone brings a cell phone and I call my mother. She is screaming and crying and I have to shout to make her understand I am all right. My father grabs the phone. He says nearly everything on that street with the tunnel entrance is gone. I try to imagine what that is like; skeleton houses, broken stones and wires ripping up the rugs and the sky coming in through the walls. Hamad. Did Hamad make it? He doesn't know. My father says that Abir needs to speak. I can't hear him very well. He tells me that he will come and get me. There is another tunnel. He will give me the information. But we must wait a few days until this stupid bombing is over. I am not to worry. I will be taken care of and if not, he, my brother, will want to know why. He makes his voice loud and I can hear how he would reach out just one long lean arm and bring me back.

I am calm and I say yes to everything. Tell our mother and father that I am fine. Tell everyone I will be back soon.

He hangs up. The calf still has its head in my armpit even though we are here in the open air. It presses close against me, shaking all over. I am also shaking all over.

Hamad must have reached the other side. Surely someone must have dug him out. Surely they found him, I am crying into the calf. I don't want Hamad to die. Maybe it's because I was too slow. *Everything on that street is gone.* If Hamad is gone, who will tell our story of the tunnel, how I imagined the gas had come, or how we saw the sunlight in the many mirrors? Who will repeat these things with me and tell Yousif, Basim and Raed that it all really happened?

For now I will have to stay on this side, in Egypt, and wait for Abir. Two other men are in this room with me. One has a broken leg and lies quietly as the other binds it up tightly. There is dirt everywhere. I settle the calf on the floor. It is hard to stand up. There is a broom by the door. I pick it up and start sweeping slowly.

This is the broom in my hands; these are my arms moving the broom, sweeping the yellow dirt into piles. Each movement hurts. Each movement says *I am here*. When Abir comes, he will hug me and that will hurt too. Maybe I will go ahead of him, in case I need to show him how we move fast in a collapsing tunnel.

SAY THAT YOU SAW BEAUTIFUL THINGS

Morning is the best time for running. Nabila says the earlier the better but I can never get my eyes open before I hear the stones against my bedroom shutter. I have to go quickly because Nabila is not patient. She will throw bigger stones and those will wake my two brothers or even Papa. Mama is already moving downstairs in the kitchen. I dress quickly and pull my *hijab* on with one hand as I push the window open with the other. The smell of last night's rain means we'll be running in the mud. No convenient tree, but Nabila has moved the ladder against the wall and I know how to come down quietly in the dark, avoiding the broken sixth-from-the-bottom rung. We carefully put the ladder back against the side of the house.

No words, no smiles, we cross the road and slip into the alleyway behind old Mrs. Dotie's house. Even if she is looking out of the window she won't say anything. She hasn't spoken since they brought back the remains of her son in a small box. They say there wasn't enough to fill a coffin, just pieces of his t-shirt and the silver bracelet from his right hand. A bomb, they say, or maybe one of those exploding bullets the police use. Amadou was ten. It wouldn't have taken much to explode him.

At the end of the alleyway, Nabila and I take it in turns to keep lookout as we slip off our veils and dresses, our tracksuits underneath. We are both 11, but I don't need the wrapping band that Nabila must use around her chest now that she's growing. She uses three safety pins to make the sure the band is tight. I have seen the red marks after she takes it off. She says it is worth it for the running. You have to see Nabila run to understand this. Even if she wasn't training for the Inter-School Olympics, she would still have to run. It is part of her, like my *oud* is part of me. I started playing *oud* when I was five and I still can't play chords like Teacher does. Chords are difficult. Posture is also difficult. Teacher whacks me on the back to make sure I sit up straight. I like the sounds my *oud* makes when I play at sunset. It is like I am playing the earth to sleep. My little brother says the sun is jumping off the earth so it doesn't have to listen to the noise.

We tie up our hair and pull on the baseball caps, checking each other to make sure no hairs are sticking out. We pile the clothes into a plastic bag and hide it under a ragged date palm crouched on the edge of the field off Shari' Surya.

And then we start. We must not take little steps that might look feminine. Nabila rolls her shoulders, runs with an easy long gait, spits into the grass. I try spitting, too, but my spit is too small and dribbles onto my chin. I use the back of my hand to wipe it away, like I have seen the football players do on TV.

She glances back at me,

— Come on, Rayan. I mean, *Ali*.

She runs faster and I keep up, following her long legs flashing ahead of me. Nabila is the fastest runner I know. To qualify for the Inter-School Olympics she must practice even though we must wear the veil all day, even though our school doesn't even have a track, and even though the protests started three days ago. Papa says it will all die down soon enough.

So, we have to be clever. Clever and careful. Because if we are caught... Hazar, the aunty from the next street, went to the market without her male chaperone. They took her away to Social Rehabilitation for three months because of the stain on her family's honor. They say terrible things happened to her at the center. They say when she came home, somehow she fell and hit her head on the bathtub. She died. Just like that.

Even though I am scared of staining my family's honor, I am here because Nabila is my best friend. We have known each other since we were too small to talk. We are sisters even if we are not related. Also, it is too dangerous for Nabila to run alone, and I am the only one who can keep up with her. Just. She is not even sprinting and I have to concentrate on making my breath smooth like she taught me. In-two-three-four-out-two-three-four. In the faint dawn light I watch her stride become longer, her legs stretching out, her whole body moving like liquid.

I must concentrate on my breathing. In-two-three, oh goodness. I am panting with my mouth open, like a dog. Fortunately, Nabila is ahead and can't see me otherwise I would be in trouble. As I make another attempt at breathing in-two-three, I crash into her because she has stopped.

I can't ask any questions because I am out of breath. Nabila is motioning with her chin at the far edge of the field. Six men are lined up like a poster for a bad movie. Black pants, white shirts. They want us to come over. Why aren't they at morning prayers? And then I see them: the black armbands with the red and green circles: the Boys of Free Ulema of Libya. If we have to speak, they will know. If they pull our hats off, they will know. We are dead.

Nabila is standing, legs apart, staring back at them. I realize they haven't yet seen we are female. We have a chance to get away if only ... But Nabila starts walking towards them. She stops and jerks her chin up. *What do you want?* We are still too far to hear what they are saying. I say quietly,

— If we run now, we can get away.

— If we run now they will follow us. Listen. Just do what I tell you. Don't speak at all. You are not able to speak. Okay?

I nod. People are always telling me I talk too much anyway.

— Now, pretend to slip and fall over.

I may talk too much but I am not clumsy. It doesn't make sense.

— Trip over. Now.

She sticks her leg behind me and I trip over her foot. I throw up my arms and we both fall over. Laughter from the boys.

— Get as much mud on you as you can.

She quickly flicks dirt onto her face. I shove my face into the red mud and feel it oozing into my hair. Nabila stands with her hands on her waist. "Look what you did, you idiot!"

Nabila's hat is tilted but her hair is still hidden. I tug my hat down with filthy hands. We slop across to the men who are still laughing. All of them are tall and have shoulders like the wrestlers on television. The leader, with a beard and a grown-together eyebrow like an angry caterpillar, holds a hand up. We are not to come too close. I stand a little behind Nabila even though I am trying to be brave.

They give us God-be-with-you and I almost give *Wa àlaykum assalam* before I remember I am to be silent. Nabila growls her greeting in a strange deep voice.

Caterpillar Eyebrow says,

— Your brother is not an athlete.

Nabila shrugs.

He nods like he is our uncle and we should respect him,

— I see you are training and that's good. But you mustn't miss morning prayers. Your father knows you are here? There are many dangers for the young.

Beneath the sludge of mud, my knees are shaking.

Another boy with a nose like it has been shut in a door, says,

— Take off the hats. We need to see your faces.

Nabila growls,

— It is the uniform. The teacher will beat us.

Caterpillar Eyebrow takes out a piece of paper,

— Never mind that. You are a good runner. I want you to take a message.

Behind her, I see Nabila's hands curled into fists. The pink nail polish I put on for her yesterday is there beneath the crust of dirt.

She says,

— But you have a phone.

Caterpillar Eyebrow's Bluetooth is the latest design. I've seen it on TV. And here it is, a smooth, black rectangle against his hairy cheek. I would like a closer look but I keep my mouth shut and my eyes down.

Caterpillar Eyebrow holds out the paper,

— Sometimes a phone is not the best way to send a message.

Nabila mustn't show her painted nails. I step forward and hold out my hand, but Caterpillar Eyebrow snatches the paper away,

— Not *you*. You would drop the message in the mud.

Flat Nose makes the stupid son-of-a-donkey joke,

—Or wipe his nose with it, *ibn-il-homaar*.

The others laugh.

I step back. Slowly, Nabila rubs one hand against the back of her shorts and holds it out palm up. Caterpillar Eyebrow gives her the paper and she immediately scrunches it into a ball and holds it against her side, fingernails tucked in. Even so, if they look closely enough they will see the pink polish with sparkles.

I can feel my heart pushing out of my throat. I cough loudly and wipe the back of my hand over my face, spreading more mud. The boys look at me and shake their heads and make comments about manners and poor upbringing. Someone says *hayawaan*. Animal.

Caterpillar Eyebrow says,

— You know the post office?

Nabili forgets to use her growly voice and it comes out too high,

— El Selmani?

Flat nose laughs,

— This one is still a girl.

Freeze.

Caterpillar Eyebrow turns on Flat Nose,

— Is it so long since your voice also came and went like his?

Behind her back, I can see Nabila's other hand, the nails digging hard into the palm.

Flat Nose jerks his chin at me,

— The other one is quiet.

Nabila's growl is back in place,

— My brother cannot speak. He is dumb.

I can see Flat Nose is ready with an insult but Caterpillar Eyebrow says,

— The dumb also have their place in Allah's plan.

He reaches out one hand and grabs the rim of my hat. I am ready to pass out when he tugs it down. He laughs. I stand still. The downward jerk has loosened the coiled-up hair. What if it comes out? I never thought my hair would get me killed. If no one asks me to look up, if I can keep my head still, the hair might stay under my hat.

— Go and find this man, Mousa. He will be at the post office with a green scarf. Give him the paper. Tell him we march in an hour.

What is this marching? Are they practicing for the army? Who is Mousa?

Caterpillar Eyebrow looks at Nabila,

— What is your name?

— Hasib.

Nabila's left leg has begun to shake. My knees are almost rattling like the small cymbals in Mamma's *riq*.

— And your father's name?

— Al Dossadi.

Flat Nose speaks up,

— I know that family.

I keep my eyes on the ground. Please don't let them ask any more questions. Please let Nabila and me go safely. I will pray every day. I will give up my new Justin Bieber poster even though I saved for three months to buy it.

Flat Nose is not ready to let us go,

— How is Hamida, the old uncle?

Nabila's voice is shaky,

— I have not seen this one.

Flat Nose shouts with laughter,

— That's because there *is* no Hamida.

Caterpillar Eyebrow shakes his head at Flat Nose and turns to Nabila,

— Now run and give the message. Don't talk to anyone on the way.

Flat Nose,

— Because if you do, we will find you.

Nabila and I turn and run towards the High School. This time I am almost faster than her. My hair is slipping, slipping, pulling against the hat. We reach the bushes near the road and my hat flies off, the hair falling out for everyone to see. Nabila pushes me to the ground. We are crouching, gasping for breath. Neither of us can move. Finally, Nabila pokes her head out, darts out and snatches up the hat.

We fix each other's hair and make sure the hats are pulled down safely. My legs are almost too shaky to stand up.

— Nabila, you are the bravest person I know. Please let us go home.

Nabila is checking her chest-band,

— How go home? We must take the message.

— But it's almost light now. People will see.

She gestures with her chin,

— *They* didn't realize. They think we are two boys on a morning run. That's all. If we don't go, they'll find us.

I look down at my muddy tracksuit. My mother will yell and Papa will probably beat me. I have a brilliant idea,

— But they *won't* get us. They'll be looking for two *boys*.

Even a beating is better than Social Rehab.

— Use your brain, Rayan. If we don't deliver the message, they'll ask questions. Then they'll find out we're not the Al Dossadis and we aren't boys. Come on. We'll just give the message to Green Scarf and go home to our loving parents.

We set off running again. Why couldn't Caterpillar Eyebrow just text like everyone else? What is so important about marching? My stomach growls. I am longing for one of Mamma's crispy rolls with milk. We run past the gas station where the trucks are lined up. The road bends east towards the clinic where the sky is leaking pale gold as we turn left for the post office. This is where the tourists come to wait for their guides to take them around the Old City. I can see a few are there already even though it is early. They wear ugly-looking pale pink and beige clothes, like they've been left out in the sun too long.

Our city is more beautiful, they say, than Tripoli. Tourists come to stay in the modern hotels and walk through the ancient city that goes back to the sixth century. They say that to see a Benghazi sunset spoils the visitors forever. They return to their own countries where their sunsets are too pale and empty.

Even though I am hungry and longing for a hot bath, I see that something looks different. On the other side of the post office, men are standing around in groups after morning prayers; but they are not going home. They are waiting for something. Some have cell-phones pressed to their ears.

At the post office there are so many people it is going to be impossible to find one green-scarf man. I am about to tell Nabila we should just give it up when we see someone standing on a low concrete wall. He is wearing the green scarf and looking around. This can't be the right Mousa: it is my music teacher, Kharim Mousa, who has taught me *oud* since I was five. I tug at Nabila but she doesn't notice. I get behind her, grateful to the crowd that moves together and apart like the waves on the beach. Teacher will see two small boys under two small hats. We finally reach him. Nabila holds out the paper and Teacher takes it. As we turn to leave, he looks at her, tries to look under the rim of my hat. I keep my face turned away and the crowd is pushing enough that Nabila and I are soon separated from him.

The post office isn't even open yet and the crowd is even bigger and noisier than usual. Can all these people be here for stamps only? Someone puts a hand on my shoulder. I spin around. An old man says,

— You boys should go home. This is no place for you.

Nabila grabs my hand and we try to push through the crowd but more people are coming and we are thrown back against a wall. Someone shouts, *Let these kids go*. A tall man swats both of us across the shoulders. *What are you doing here? Go home to your parents*. Nabila stumbles to her knees and her hat falls off. I throw myself across her and both of us fall to the ground. I grab her hat and jam it on her head. No one has seen. No one is paying attention. Everyone is talking and texting. *Did you hear? Is it starting?*

My teacher, Kharim Mousa is lifted high into the air. He shouts. It takes a long time before people start listening. He is saying strange things,

— The time has come, brothers. We must be prepared to face the worst. We must be free. The men are cheering, raising clenched fists in the air. Nabila and I could take all our clothes off and no one would notice.

The crowd begins to move away from the post office. Teacher is among them. The crowd begins to move out to the First Ring Road and we are pulled along with them. We hold hands. We mustn't be separated. As the crowd walks, they chant. No one is chanting the same thing and I can only make out some of the words.

Nabila and I try to wriggle out of the crowd to cross the road, but more people come and we are pressed back. Someone grabs my arm and I hold on to Nabila. The crowd is no longer the sea but a hungry monster, pressing us apart with its many arms and many legs. Everyone breathes in the same air together. They breathe in again and a large man moves forward, ignoring our joined hands. He pushes between us, and Nabila's hand slips from mine. I can't even call out.

I hang on to my hat as I am sucked back and forth. I am finally ejected and I stumble against broken concrete. My knee is bleeding and I sit on the curb to catch my breath and wipe off the blood. I will never find Nabila now. And what am I going to tell my parents?

Behind me someone is talking in English. I turn around and see a small man in the brown uniform of the Al-Nooran Hotel guides, his metal name tag a faint glow in the dim light. He hasn't seen me. He is standing very straight, waving one arm, but I can't see who he is talking to.

— Sir, madam. There is no problem. All is safe here. Just a few young hotheads. Allow me to take you to the Old City. Let us not dwell on this little disturbance. We will create the proper memories of the real Benghazi, the jewel of North Africa. We can say that you saw beautiful things.

He clears his throat. He starts again,

— Sir, madam. There is no problem …

He breaks off as two tourists approach: a skinny, bald man holds an umbrella over his wife's head even though the sun is barely up. The small man hurries over and beckons them to the waiting car.

In the growing light, I can see Teacher walking towards me, his green scarf now draped over the head of someone he is carrying in his arms. Nabila. I am up and running, despite the throbbing knee. Is she dead?

He falls to his knees as I reach him and I sit so that I can cradle Nabila's head in my arms. Under the scarf there are dark bruises down one side of her face. Her eyes are shut.

— *Nabila*.

Her tracksuit is covered in dirt. I want to see if there are other wounds but Teacher puts out a hand. I must not uncover her in public.

He stands up,

— I will find a taxi. We must get her to the hospital.

Her chest lifts and falls quickly in half-breaths. Is she bleeding under the tracksuit? Teacher returns,

— Rayan, what foolishness is this? Don't you realize you could have been arrested?

There are long scratches down Nabila's neck that disappear beneath her shirt.

Teacher slowly breathes in and out. It is the same breathing for when I make mistakes in my lesson,

— They discovered she is a girl. You are dressed like *boys*, Rayan. People cannot tolerate this kind of behavior, this deception. She is lucky they only gave her a few slaps. It could have been worse.

What slaps can leave these marks? I don't want to think about *worse*,

— They didn't have to hurt her. What did she do to them?

But Teacher is looking towards the city,

— Rayan, we are fighting for our freedom. It is our turn. We are doing this for our country.

His words are for them, some nameless crowd of men marching up and down. He waves his arms as he sees a taxi.

Nabila moves her lips. I can see she is trying to say my name. I touch her hair gently,

— Nabila, I am here.

Together, Teacher and I lift Nabila into the back of the taxi. I carefully slide in beside her. Even Social Rehabilitation would be better than seeing Nabila so silent, her breathing so shallow. Teacher sits in front with the driver.

As we drive away, I hear jeers, shouts and the smashing of glass. Someone calls through a megaphone. Teacher turns towards the sound. He begins to open the window and then rolls it shut. The shouting reaches a triumphant climax as I hear the first round of gunshots. I put my hand over Nabila's eyes.

JEWELS WE TOOK WITH US

At school our teachers warned us about the foolishness of those who trusted their lives to boats. They unrolled the colored map of the world. Here is Morocco, our country. Here is Spain, their country. Here is the port with many guards who shoot at anyone who tries to cross the sea. Here is the shifting sea, waiting to suck you down into darkness.

Harraq. That's what people called us: the ones who were running, the ones who were temporary. Street kids.

Lucee's plan: we will go to her aunt's place in Tangier. The aunt will shelter us for a few days. Then we will take a boat to Malaga where men worship the women and buy cakes for them and some even do the cooking. None of us can imagine that.

Maybe we will save up and buy a house together, the four of us.

Malaga is the most beautiful place in the world.

None of us have been on a boat. None of us understands how to drive the boat. None of us knows where Malaga is. But ever since we saw the *Holidays In Spain* show on Mrs. Hosni's TV, that's where we want to go.

December 2011

Being us is the best in the world. Lucee is sixteen. Mouna and Batoul are fifteen. Me, Yasmine, I am thirteen.

Mouna asks how far Tangier is from our village.

Mouna is small, like me, but she is tough. She can beat me at arm-wrestling. She has a pretty nose, one of those girls who is pretty even when she is scratching her legs.

My nose bends over like a hunchback. I am not pretty. The husband says the only reason he married me is because I'm young and can bear children. He is looking for a better woman.

Batoul says she can steal her brother's motorbike. But how will we all fit on? Batoul is tall with glasses. She is the third wife because her husband wanted more kids. The first wife is okay but the second wife is cruel to Batoul and steals her food. I try to bring bread for Batoul. She is always hungry.

Lucee has a dimple in her right cheek and we see it all the time when she laughs. Lucee is my best friend and she takes care of me.

Me,

— We don't know the way. We will be lost and eaten by wild dogs.

Lucee, dimple flashing, laughs.

— No wild dogs will eat us. We will eat *them*.

January 2012

We left at New Year. As always, the husbands went to a bar in the next village. The beer was homemade and very strong, so the men would sleep all day. Most would wake up the next day and start drinking again. They gave money to the butcher who cooked food for them. The women, of course, stayed at home, waiting for the arrival of the drunk husbands. But this time, these wives wouldn't be waiting.

We met at the swinging tree near the river, like we planned.

We each had a small bag or a scarf to hold some clothes and the money we'd taken from the house. Each of us brought a knife. Lucee's was big, for cutting up meat. Mine was so small that it looked like a pen.

Mouna's tummy was still flat. Batoul's looked like a new moon. Lucee's was the biggest but she wore a loose tunic over her pants.

We needed to walk far before we dared to find a truck to give us a ride.

Batoul had stolen a Morocco map from the second wife. We saw that we could follow the main road. After two hours of walking on the forest path, we crept nearer to the road.

We had all seen this, the men who waved at trucks to get a ride. We shyly waved at the first truck but it thundered past.

Batoul,

— We should go back to the forest. We should go home.

Lucee,

— Batoul, you can't go home. Your husband will kill you. And then you will have caused the death of your baby.

Batoul cried out. We put our arms around her and clicked our tongues at Lucee.

We understood why Lucee said this. We'd come this far and we couldn't turn back. But it was too much for Batoul to take the death of her baby on her soul.

Another truck, with rattling milk cans in the back. Mouna waved. The truck stopped. Mouna and I climbed in first and helped the others up. We leaned against the milk cans. We hardly dared to look at each other and then we started laughing. Even Batoul. We were on a truck!

Now the journey had really started.

November 2011

Sometimes we rebel against the husbands. Mouna puts a little dog blood in her husband's soup. Lucee grinds up cockroaches and puts them in her husband's favorite dessert. Batoul soaks her husband's prayer cap in goat pee. She washes it with the strong detergent we all use, but there is the smallest smell left that will come to him as he kneels for his prayers. We whisper these stories and laugh as we do the washing. We are still the leopard-girls that were at school just last year.

I add goat feces to the husband's stew. He finds out. He kicks me to the ground, cracks my ribs, chokes me, and says he will pull my head off. He is an important man. He can do anything.

I have two black eyes, my left arm is broken and there are marks around my neck. I walk slowly for a month. The others help me with the washing so the husband won't beat me again. We tell jokes.

All the stories we tell won't change anything. We are like this because our mothers are like this. We are like this until the husbands die, or we die.

January 2012

It was late afternoon when we got down just outside Rabat. None of us had been this far from home. We wanted to see the city, the wide streets and big buildings that went up twenty stories high. But there was no time to be tourists.

The afternoon was growing shadows. We were talking about using some of our precious dirham on bus fare when a green van stopped. A woman leaned out,

— Where to?

We piled into her van. It was full of bags of knitted blue and pink and yellow and white. Baby clothes. We all became tearful, even me, and touched the small jackets and pants, the dresses.

— So, girls, you are visiting family?

Me,

— Yes, madam. Tangier, madam.

Lucee was holding a tiny blanket. Weeping.

The driver looked in the rearview mirror.

— Your baby is coming soon, sister? Your family must be very happy. Don't worry. I know how it is. You want to visit but the uncle can't make it, the brother is off with his friends, the father is working. If we have to wait for men to help us where would we be? I started this business myself six years ago. Got tired of waiting for my no-good husband to do something.

I wanted to know more. Maybe this was a way we could make money in Malaga,

— You made all these yourself?

She laughed,

— Not me. Can't knit. My sister, my cousins. We sold among our neighbors and then at the market. We bought softer wool, some silk even. This is an order for a customer in Algiers.

Lucee,

— And your husband?

The driver laughed and smacked the steering wheel.

— Left him a long time ago. I send him money sometimes so he won't give me any trouble. I live with my sister.

She shook her head.

— You are all so young. So young.

We stopped near a marketplace just outside Tangier, and we thanked her. She gave Lucee a white bonnet for the baby. I could see the others were thinking of the small lives growing inside.

The driver touched my arm.

— Don't speak to anyone else until you reach your aunt's house.

October 2010

We are not finished with school when we are married, boom, boom, boom, boom. Just like that. All within the same year, like the husbands planned it.

With us, girls get married, even the ones who want to go to university, even the ones with big noses or glasses. Husbands like young wives. Between the husbands-rights part and the beating part, there is not much to choose. But our mothers have done it, and *their* mothers, and *their* mothers, so we must also do it.

I bet those modern women in Tangier go to university. I bet no one tells them when to get married.

At the river, we wash the clothes, sleeves rolled, skirts tucked up. We see the bruises, the bumps on elbows and shins. Sometimes one of us moves more slowly and we know: fractured ribs, wrists, fingers. A bandage wrapping shows from under sleeves. Somehow the husbands know not to damage legs because we won't be able to clean or cook. Batoul walks slowly more often. Her husband is very important in the village.

And then they are all pregnant. Boom, boom, boom. Like that. One moment Lucee is pale and sweating, then Batoul is vomiting, then Mouna has a headache. They say, *It will happen to you, too.*

I didn't know twelve was old enough to be married. The husband gave my father 1000 dirham for me. Boom. Married.

Tangier. Men everywhere. *You are children. You cannot come here. You are a curse. Where is your father, your mother?*

Most of them, when they saw Lucee was pregnant, they left us alone. It was good we were four.

We couldn't look for Lucee's aunt because it was evening, and everything turned to dark shapes that changed as we passed. We wanted to step into a house with a door to close. We wanted to drink tea, lie on mats, listen to the outside city sounds and feel ourselves falling asleep.

But there was nothing to do except look for a place to rest until morning. After inspecting three alleyways, one with a headless dog, we found a space behind a clothing store next to a pile of broken boxes. We cleared the plastic bags and papers away and pulled the boxes around us.

Mouna and me were keeping watch when the man came.

— You are far from your home, I think. You had better come with me.

He thought we were foolish girls who could do nothing. But we had seen women in our village beaten just because they spoke when they were told to be silent. We had been beaten by our husbands for less, and we were not about to be beaten by a stranger.

Mouna and me, we took out our knives.

The man looked at us, and laughed. He lunged for Mouna and she stabbed his hand. He tried to get her knife and I stabbed him in the leg. He was shouting and so were we. Lucee sat on his stomach. I sat on his legs. Batoul hit him with a piece of wood and he stopped shouting.

Kids came running. *What has happened? Is dead?*

The skinny teenage boy with oil-black eyes,

— Come.

He didn't even look to see if we followed. He slipped out from the alleyway and behind a row of stalls. Mouna grabbed his shirt as he turned the corner.

— Where are we going?

— You need somewhere to stay, yes? I can show you a safe place.

September 2009

Lucee and me running through the field with Aunty Hannah chasing us because we stole two of her eggs. Aunty is screaming. We are laughing so hard we can barely run through Aunty's yard and onto the path that goes through the forest. We come out near Lucee's house and sit on a log, kicking our heels and drinking up the eggs. My mother used to cook them when she was with us.

Mouna and Batoul don't care about school. They just want to get married. But me and Lucee we're going to university. I'm eleven and I know marriage is for losers.

Lucee's mother also died, like mine, but not from beating. She died having Lucee's brother. He died also. They buried him at the back of the house. That's a good place for a dead baby. Babies are too little to have a ceremony. I don't want a ceremony when I die, either. I want to just fly up into the air and be with all the other dead people. Like my mother.

January 2012

We weren't sure about following the boy but we didn't want to stay behind in the alley.

He led us away from the stalls, from the main streets, to where the houses were smaller, leaning against each other. Blue plastic covered the windows, rusty-looking metal sheets over the roofs, clothes hanging, looped along the walls.

The streets began to slope downhill. What if we were going into a dangerous place? How would we be able to escape uphill, especially Lucee?

The streets ended. Just like that. We were in an open place, like a giant pounded the earth flat. Cracked and rusted metal spokes lay ready to stab you in the leg. A concrete building so old you couldn't tell what was window and what was just hole. The holes were leaning against very wobbly-looking scaffolding. And the boy headed straight for it.

Me,

— I'm not going up there.

Together, Manou and Batoul pulled me from bar to bar, *ohgodohgodohgodohgod*, all the way up.

Lucee came up last and shook me,

— Shh. They are looking.

Kids with large eyes and skinny legs. One said we shouldn't have come. The boy told them to be quiet.

He held out his hand. Mouna gave him 10 dirham. He kept his hand open. She gave him 10 more.

— Down there. The room at the end. It has a hole in the floor. The window side.

None of us slept, except Lucee. And in the morning I was glad to stand up.

Tangier went on as far as you could see. We walked and walked through the streets that went up and down and around, but Lucee's aunt was nowhere. We walked through the markets where the tinsmiths bang-banged, past the antique sellers, past the heaps of painted pigs, embroidered cushion covers, sheepskins, wooden washboards that the tourists so loved. We coughed past the perfume makers.

Batoul stood like a statue in front of the slipper shop where the shoes were covered in jewels. We had to pull her away.

We parted with precious dirham to buy soap. Imperial Leather. We took turns breathing in the delicious smell. We rescued half a Mariah Carey t-shirt from a cardboard box to use as a washcloth.

Each day in Tangier meant more money we had to spend on orange juice for 5dh, eggplant and rice 7dh, bread and honey 5dh, and chickpea cakes 2dh. We said, *How delicious*. But we were still hungry. It was difficult sharing one portion between four, all of us saying, *No, no. I am full. Lucee, can you eat for me?*

We learned to hide the money on different parts of our bodies.

We learned to hide our bodies behind the stalls, in doorways, against parked cars.

We learned to watch.

I learned to climb the scaffolding without fear. Almost.

We walked up and down the twisting streets and Lucee's aunt was still nowhere.

We slept pressed against the wall in our room, scared that the police would come, that the husbands would come, that we would fall through the hole and die. The fear came roaring out of our dreams and woke us throughout the night, sobbing, whispering. Once, they told me, I screamed.

On the third evening, Batoul began to cry.

Mouna,

— What is it? You are hurt?

— No.

— Then?

Batoul,

— The slippers. The red ones with the blue jewels.

Lucee,

— I wanted the blue ones with the white jewels on the heel.

Mouna,

— Don't cry, Batoul. When we are in Malaga, you will have many jeweled slippers.

August 2008

Lucee's thirteenth birthday. We spy on the new neighbors-in-the-next-street. They have four boys. They also have a girl. Batoul. We like her name. Like a warrior. All afternoon we play being Batoul and the dragon. Batoul kills the dragon every time.

When we finally talk to her, though, she has a soft voice. Not a warrior at all. She likes to read books, like me. Lucee says that's why she wears glasses. She will never get married because husbands don't like glasses. I'm not getting married anyway. Lucee says she's not getting married, either.

January 2012

The man in the alley. I pushed a knife through the pants and into the leg. I didn't know that blood came thick like that. It took a long time to wash his blood out of our clothes. And even then you could see the stains, the outlines of what we'd done.

We knew about the smuggling gangs, the men who killed because you didn't arrange the boat with them, or you didn't have the money. Or they might kill you even if you had the money. There was nothing we could do about them. We had to turn our minds away from these thoughts of killing.

The boy said he would help us find a boat. We had to trust him.

July 2007

Mouna is late to the river. Her mother is sick again so Mouna has to do all the work. Her father will beat her if she doesn't finish.

Lucee says that when the mother is ill like this, the father makes Mouna be the wife.

January 2012

All of us were talking about the things we loved: the yoghurt, the bread, our own blankets, even mine with the burned edge because the husband said that's all I deserved. But it was mine and I loved it. The burned edge was like a path and sometimes I followed it with my finger, right off the end of the blanket, right into the sky winking at me through the hole in the roof, right into Switzerland and Sweden and all those places we learned about at school.

We were crying.

Suddenly, the boy was there in our doorway with six other kids looking over his shoulder.

Mouna,

— What is it?

The six kids began talking over each other,

You said they would leave. Why are they still here?

We argued. They argued back. Each voice was jumping on top of every other voice. The empty building threw back our voices over and over.

The boy picked up a stick and beat one of the metal panels. We all stopped.

— I have a boat for you.

We stared at him. He looked at each of us,

— You want a boat, yes?

A boat. For us.

I said,

— How much?

He laughed.

— I will tell you when we reach the boat.

Mouna grabbed his arm just as he turned to walk off. She spoke quietly so the other kids couldn't hear.

— You know we don't have money.

He looked like he'd lived in this building all his life.

— Bring what you have.

His oil-black eyes didn't look at us but through us to some other place.

June 2006

I'm eight and I'm big enough to do the washing at the river. But Mouna and me are throwing water at Lucee who has her eyes shut tight and is splashing with both arms like a crazy windmill. Half the clothes are washed. The other clothes still lie in piles, waiting for our hard-working hands and arms. But for now we are squealing and soaked.

Batoul moves away from us. The last time we did this, her father took away Batoul's food for two days. *If you have time to play when you should be working, then you don't need to eat.*

I call her,

— Batoul! Help us!

But she moves away downstream. She is too thin. She can't miss meals.

January 2012

I found him smoking a pipe, sitting on the ledge of a broken out window.

— You are going to lead us into a trap. You are going to let those smugglers take us.

I had my arms folded. It was all I could think of to do to make my heart stop beating so quickly.

Slowly, he swung his legs around and faced me.

— I found a boat. You need one. You will give me money for it. That's all.

— Why do you help us?

— Listen. Your friend is going to have a baby. She can't have it here.

His eyes looked past me,

— I once knew ... I once had a—

He stood up and leaned against the wall. His pipe had gone out,

— It's up to you. If you don't want the boat, I can sell it to someone else.

At midnight, the boy came for us and we walked far out of Tangier. Mouna and Lucee were carrying bread and tomatoes. It was raining.

This was lucky, the boy said. People wouldn't try to cross when it rained.

We had looked at Batoul's map, at the narrow section of sea between our country and Spain. We had heard it took nine hours, fifteen hours, two days. We heard the guards arrested everyone, shot at the boats, left people to drown.

The boy said we would go at night, and take a route farther out of town. He told us we would have to carry our boat two kilometers to the shore. After that we would have to escape the guards and the boat smugglers who were everywhere.

May 2005

Lucee and me are walking to the traveling market in the next village. My mother says, *Go on, make the most of it. These days aren't going to last.*

It's going to be perfect. Lucee's father is gone to Sefrou to sit with his friends in the bar. He won't be back until tomorrow.

Early this morning, we fetched water, swept, made the beds, fed the kids, and scoured out the breakfast pots.

We even have a few dirham for ourselves. From the travelers, I am to buy spices that my mother can't get in the village. But Lucee and me can spend the leftover coins.

Lucee,

— What are you going to buy?

— What are *you* going to buy?

Lucee's face goes tight with excitement,

— Red slippers.

— Maroon 5 poster.

We look at each other,

— *What?*

Lucee is laughing so hard I have to punch her to make her stop.

— *Ow.* They won't have any Maroon 5 poster.

— They *will*. They have *everything*.

— Listen, stupid. They have food and clothes.

Lucee grabs my arm,

— Don't be mad, Yasmine. They have food and clothes only. And where would you put the poster anyway?

She's right. Maybe I'll get red slippers, too. They're easier to hide.

January 2012

We walked through the black bones of night, away from the streets, across paths and onto no-path-land. We walked until there were no more buildings. We walked in and out of the forest. I tried not to think about the demon story Lucee once told me that made me pee my pants.

We came to a house that had broken walls and no door. Inside was a pile of branches and canvas. The boat was beneath. We never thought to see a boat hidden like this.

The boy showed us how to use the foot pump and make sure each section of the dinghy was hard with air.

We gave him one hundred and twenty dirham. Nearly all our money.

He gave Lucee the foot pump and the rest of us carried the boat out of the house. It was heavy but we were used to carrying water and wet laundry. We moved quickly towards the trees. The boy said that after we passed through the forest there would be two hills and then the sea.

He stopped and motioned us to be still.

Then he told us to run. *They are coming*.

We yanked the boat up and raced to the safe trees, the boat bumping between us, Lucee panting behind with the pump. We turned around. The boy wasn't with us.

We peered between the branches. Back near the house, maybe a hundred meters away, he was held between two men. We saw their outlines. They pulled at him like they were in a film. We saw him shake his head.

He died right in front of us. Even with the gunshot, I didn't realize he was dead until I saw him fall, his legs folding under him like he was sitting to smoke his pipe.

We picked up our boat and ran. The trees were good cover, but we had to make it over the hills to the beach. It was rocky there, the boy had said, and if there were guards we could hide until we were able to put the dinghy in the water.

We ran through the hammering rain. I kept shouting *lift* as we forced our way between the gouging thorn bushes. Lucee wanted to pee. We told her to pee while she was running.

The boat got heavier. My legs felt like they were going to give up.

And the boy, suddenly so small between the two men, his legs folding underneath him.

Two hills? We went up and down at least six. We dragged that boat over the last hill and finally saw the sea. We crouched by the rocks while Mouna checked for guards. No white lights flashed across the rain-bitten water. No dogs barked. No one shouted. It was as the boy said: no one crossed from this place.

We hoisted the boat up again and started moving slowly across the wet rocks. We called to each other to be careful. I don't remember how we got the boat down to the rough sand at the water's edge.

Even then, with the rain beating at us, and our fear of the guards and the two men, Mouna made us inflate the boat properly with the foot pump.

April 2004

A short girl with a pretty nose is upside down in our swinging tree.

— I'm Mouna. My aunt has a bakery. You like fresh bread?

Lucee and me are always ready for fresh bread. The bakery is a new shop on the far side of the village.

The aunt is busy with customers so we wait outside while Mouna gets us two rolls. The aunt also makes cakes. Mouna says she will steal some for us.

Lucee and me are impressed.

January 2012

The boy had said to count the waves so we could catch the one that would take us out, but we were too scared to wait. We pushed our boat into the water. The waves kept shoving us back in. And then we realized that if three got in and one pushed we could get the boat out further.

I was the only one not pregnant. Lucee wanted to help but I was afraid she'd hurt the baby. Lucee sat behind Mouna and Batoul who were holding the paddles.

Lucee put my hand on her stomach. I felt a small nudging under my fingers, like the tiniest foot was waving hello. Lucee smiled. Her face was beautiful. I wondered if I might become beautiful if I had a baby.

I tried not to think about poisonous jellyfish, or the barracuda that ripped mouthfuls as they swam like lightning, or the coast guards whose white lights could easily catch us, and how we might end up like the boy folding his legs as he fell.

I tried to think of beautiful Malaga, where there were cakes and melons and enough tomatoes and bread for everyone.

I wanted to swim us to Spain so the babies would grow up with fruit in each hand.

I tried not to think about the fact that I couldn't swim. None of us could.

It was still raining hard. I kept walking the boat out, the water now past my knees, up to my waist, up to my armpits. I could feel the water pulling me, and the small stones under my feet.

March 2003

I open my fist. It is a pink stone for Lucee. She opens her fist. It is a yellow stone for me. This is the first gift I have ever had. It is so beautiful I can't move. We sit under the swinging tree and tell the story of the girl who flies over the ocean. The pink stone is the girl. The yellow stone is the sun shining a golden path across the sea. We put our stones in the small forest pool near Lucee's house. We can come and hold them each day. We can see the colors shining up at us and they will always be these bright jewels in the water.

Acknowledgements

I would like to thank the following journals for first giving these stories a home:

30 Below: Spring edition 2011, Battered Suitcase,

Say That You Saw Beautiful Things: October 2011, Lightship Publishing Anthology (finalist Lightship Publishing Short Story Competition)   .

Jewels We Took With Us: September 2014, Chicago Tribune (finalist Nelson Algren Award)

About the author

Sandra Hunter's fiction has been published in a number of literary magazines and received the October 2014 Africa Book Club Award, 2014 H.E. Francis Fiction Award, 2012 Cobalt Fiction Prize, and three Pushcart Prize nominations. Her debut novel, *Losing Touch*, was released in July 2014 (OneWorld Publications). When she's not working on her second novel, *The Geography of Kitchen Tables*, she teaches English and Creative Writing at Moorpark College and runs writing workshops in Ventura and Los Angeles. Favorite dessert: rose-flavored macarons.